Welcome to ALADDIN QUIX!

If you are looking for fast, fun-to-read stories with colorful characters, lots of kid-friendly humor, easy-to-follow action, entertaining story lines, and lively illustrations, then **ALADDIN QUIX** is for you!

But wait, there's more!

If you're also looking for stories with tables of contents; word lists; about-the-book questions; 64, 80, or 96 pages; short chapters; short paragraphs; and large fonts, then **ALADDIN QUIX** is *definitely* for you!

ALADDIN QUIX: The next step between ready to reads and longer, more challenging chapter books, for readers five to eight years old.

Read more ALADDIN QUIX books!

By Stephanie Calmenson

Our Principal Is a Frog!
Our Principal Is a Wolf!
Our Principal's in His Underwear!
Our Principal Breaks a Spell!
Our Principal's Wacky Wishes!

Royal Sweets
By Helen Perelman

Book 1: *A Royal Rescue*
Book 2: *Sugar Secrets*
Book 3: *Stolen Jewels*
Book 4: *The Marshmallow Ghost*
Book 5: *Chocolate Challenge*

A Miss Mallard Mystery
By Robert Quackenbush

Dig to Disaster
Texas Trail to Calamity
Express Train to Trouble
Stairway to Doom
Bicycle to Treachery
Gondola to Danger
Surfboard to Peril
Taxi to Intrigue

Little Goddess Girls
By Joan Holub and Suzanne Williams

Book 1: *Athena & the Magic Land*
Book 2: *Persephone & the Giant Flowers*
Book 3: *Aphrodite & the Gold Apple*
Book 4: *Artemis & the Awesome Animals*
Book 5: *Athena & the Island Enchantress*
Book 6: *Persephone & the Evil King*
Book 7: *Aphrodite & the Magical Box*

Little GODDESS Girls

Artemis & the Wishing Kitten

JOAN HOLUB & SUZANNE WILLIAMS

ALADDIN QUIX

New York London Toronto Sydney New Delhi

ALADDIN QUIX
Simon & Schuster Children's Publishing Division
1230 Avenue of the Americas, New York, New York 10020
First Aladdin QUIX hardcover edition September 2021
Text copyright © 2021 by Joan Holub and Suzanne Williams
Illustrations copyright © 2021 by Yuyi Chen
Also available in an Aladdin QUIX paperback edition.
All rights reserved, including the right of reproduction in whole or in part in any form.
ALADDIN and the related marks and colophon are trademarks of Simon & Schuster, Inc.
For information about special discounts for bulk purchases, please contact
Simon & Schuster Special Sales at 1-866-506-1949 or business@simonandschuster.com.
The Simon & Schuster Speakers Bureau can bring authors to your live event. For more information or to book an event contact the Simon & Schuster Speakers Bureau at 1-866-248-3049 or visit our website at www.simonspeakers.com.
Designed by Tiara Iandiorio
The illustrations for this book were rendered digitally.
The text of this book was set in Archer Medium.
Manufactured in the United States of America 0821 LAK
2 4 6 8 10 9 7 5 3 1
Library of Congress Control Number 2021931178
ISBN 978-1-5344-7969-2 (hc)
ISBN 978-1-5344-7968-5 (pbk)
ISBN 978-1-5344-7970-8 (ebook)

Cast of Characters

Artemis (AR•tuh•miss): Black-haired Greek goddess of hunting and animals

Athena (uh•THEE•nuh): Brown-haired Greek goddess of wisdom

Persephone (purr•SEFF•uh•nee): Red-haired Greek goddess of plants and flowers

Aphrodite (af•row•DIE•tee): Golden-haired Greek goddess of love and beauty

Oliver (AH•liv•er): Athena's white puppy

Hestia (HESS•tee•uh): A small, winged Greek goddess who helps Athena and her friends

Prince Paris (PRINTZ PAR•iss): A boy who wants Helen the kitten for his pet

Zeus (ZOOSS): Most powerful of the Greek gods, who lives in Sparkle City and can grant wishes

Odysseus (oh•DISS•ee•uss): A boy who wants to take Helen the kitten back to his king

Helen (HELL•uhn): A pink kitten with green eyes

Pigasus (PIG•uh•suss): A flying pig that says poems

Contents

1

New Tricks

Zing! **Artemis** shot a magic silver arrow from her bow. It sailed away. High in the air it did a loop-the-loop! Just as she had taught it to do.

Her three best friends **Athena,**

Persephone, and **Aphrodite** were all safely behind her. The four girls, and Athena's little white dog, **Oliver**, were walking on the orange, blue, and pink Hello Brick Road.

Up ahead they could see rainbow-colored sparkles coming from Sparkle City. That was where they were heading. They'd been invited to a pet show there! The city was only a few minutes away now, at the very top of magical **Mount Olympus**.

After it finished its loop-the-loop, Artemis's arrow came to a stop in the air. Then it zoomed down to land way ahead of everyone on the otherwise empty brick road. *Clack!*

"Go, boy! Fetch!"

Artemis yelled to Oliver.

"Woof!" Leaving Athena's side, the little dog dashed off to get the arrow.

When he found it, he grabbed it in his mouth. He ran over to Artemis and proudly dropped it at her feet. She picked it up. Then she put it back in the long, thin **quiver** she carried over one shoulder.

"Good job," she told the dog as she patted his head. She liked teaching him tricks. But the most important thing was that he liked doing them!

Persephone, Aphrodite, and Athena clapped for him. **"Good boy!" "Yay, Oliver!" "Woo-hoo!"** they called.

Even the magic sandals Athena wore acted like they were proud of him. Their wings flapped as if they were clapping, lifting her off the ground a few inches. Athena had gotten the sandals not long ago, before Artemis had met her.

Excited by everyone's **praise**, Oliver began chasing his tail. Then he rolled around on his back in a patch of clover by the side of the road. A clover got stuck on his wet nose. The girls laughed at how silly he looked as he shook it off.

Artemis was so happy to be

with her friends. As they contin-
ued to walk, she thought about
how different the four of them
were.

But they were alike in one
very important way. They were
all **goddess** girls! A tiny flying
goddess named **Hestia** had told
them that. They were each still
learning to use their special
powers.

The girls also all liked having
adventures together. During their
last adventure, a magic elevator

had taken them to the three Lands of Boo-Boo. They'd met some very strange creatures on the trip, including a **curious**, talking box named Pandora!

Oliver trotted back onto the road and over to the girls. "You look pooped. Want a ride?" Athena asked him. She scooped him up in her arms. He licked her chin and wiggled around. Then he snuggled in for a nap.

Athena smiled over at Artemis. "Oliver's getting pretty good at

the tricks you're teaching him."

Artemis smiled back. She reached over to rub the dog's head. "Yeah. He's really fun."

Though Oliver was Athena's dog, whenever Athena went back home, she let Artemis take care of him. Because unlike the other girls, Athena didn't belong in this magic land. A strange storm had blown her to Mount Olympus from her home far away. She had met Oliver here, and they'd become pals.

By now, the girls were getting close to Sparkle City. It was surrounded by a high glass wall dotted with sparkly jewels. And the wall had no door or gate! Luckily, Aphrodite had found a magic apple on one of their adventures. It was the key to passing through the wall.

Oliver had begun to wiggle, so Athena set him down. He ran ahead, up to a boy with brown hair wearing a crown. The boy was standing on the road holding a pink kitten!

2

The Pink Kitten

Oliver ran around the new boy on the Hello Brick Road a few times. Then the dog dashed off into the grass to chase butterflies.

"Hi! I'm **Prince Paris**," the boy told the girls when they came up to him. "I live in Sparkle City. Is this your kitten? I found her just now on the road. Her collar doesn't have a name tag."

"Oh no! She must be lost!" said Artemis.

"I guess so," said the boy. He petted the kitten, and it snuggled against him. The kitten's eyes were as green as emeralds.

"I'll take her if you want," said Artemis. She reached over and petted the kitten too. "I like animals."

This was true. But Artemis used to be scared of animals, as well as many other things. She'd even been scared of Oliver at first. But **Zeus**, the king of the **gods**, had given her a ruby heart. It helped remind her to feel brave.

Paris grinned at the pink kitten. "Thanks, but I think I'll keep her," he said to Artemis. "She's so cute."

Suddenly another boy with red hair came running up the road. **"Hey!"** he called to the girls and Paris. "I'm **Odysseus** from the city of Sparta. I'm looking for a pink kitten who belongs to my king. I was bringing her to the Sparkle City pet show. But she ran off. Her name is **Helen**."

Odysseus did not see the kitten right away. Paris and the girls had their backs to him. But now they all turned to Odysseus.

Odysseus **gasped** and pointed at the kitten. **"That's her!"** He tried to take the kitten.

Paris shook his head and backed away. "This kitten must

not like your king if she ran off," he told Odysseus. "Maybe he didn't take good care of her. I will, though. Helen is mine now."

"My king did take care of her. So did I. Losing her was an **accident**. You have no right to keep her!" said Odysseus.

"**Hmph!** Finders keepers," said Paris.

He turned and ran to the glass wall. There was a tall lady standing by it. She was holding a gold apple in one hand. After looking at the kitten, she nodded to Paris. "You and your pet may enter," she said.

She touched her apple against the glass wall. The wall began to ripple. Then the boy stepped through the wall and disappeared into Sparkle City.

3

Sparkle City

"**Pet show!** Line up here if you want to enter Sparkle City," the lady by the wall called out.

Odysseus left the girls and raced over to her. But the lady wouldn't let him in. "Step aside," she said as the girls caught up to him. "Only those with pets are allowed inside the city."

There were many food and water bowls set out for pets along the wall. Oliver ran over to eat and drink from them. There were also snacks for the visitors who had traveled here for the show. The girls went over, grabbed some, and began munching.

Meanwhile, three more people came up to the wall. They grabbed snacks too. Then they got in line with their pets. One boy's pet was a ferret in a tutu. Another pet was a poodle with two fancy pom-pom tails. And a third pet was a raccoon that was juggling nuts!

The lady wrote each pet's name on a list she held. Then she

let them and their owners pass through the wall and into the city.

The goddess girls finished off their snacks, then got in line too. Odysseus came to stand by them.

Is he going to try to sneak in with us since he doesn't have a pet of his own? Artemis wondered.

"Whose dog is that?" the lady asked when it was the girls' turn. She pointed at Oliver.

"He's mine," said Athena.

"Then you may enter the city with him," said the lady. "However, your friends can't come in, since they don't have pets."

"But I have a gold apple," said Aphrodite.

The lady shook her head. "Sorry. Special rules for the pet show. Your gold apple key won't work today. Only mine will. Zeus is being extra careful about who comes in. Just so there's no trouble to **spoil** the fun."

"I have a magic silver cane. **Will it work as a key?**" asked Persephone. She showed the lady her cane. She'd gotten it after they'd all saved a queen from an evil spell not long ago.

The lady shook her head again. "No. I'm sorry."

"But Zeus himself invited the four of us," Artemis huffed. This had happened when the girls came upon him during their recent adventure in the Lands of Boo-Boo.

"Hmm. What are your names?" the lady asked the goddess girls.

When they told her, she said, "Ah yes. Zeus told me you are his special guests. You four girls may go into Sparkle City."

"I'm with them," Odysseus told the lady.

She looked at the girls. "Do you know him?"

"Sort of. We met him on the Hello Brick Road," said Athena.

"Not good enough," the lady told Odysseus. "You can't come in. Not if you don't have a pet."

"But my king sent me to enter his kitten in the pet show," Odysseus told her. He explained what had happened with Paris, but the lady wouldn't listen. "Please move. Others are waiting to get in." She pointed to the long line behind them.

"**Next!**" she called to a boy. His pet was a blue pig with wings!

"We'll be back in a minute," Artemis told the lady. She pulled Odysseus and her friends out of line.

"I have an idea to get Odysseus into the city," Artemis told her friends. To him, she said, "But you have to promise you won't start trouble once you're inside."

He nodded. "I won't. But Paris must give me the kitten. Helen is very special. My king **adores** her. If I return home without her, I will be in big trouble! So what's your idea?"

"Well, how about if you *make* a pet to enter in the show?" Artemis suggested.

Aphrodite's eyes lit up. She pointed to some tree branches lying in the grass. "Yeah! Maybe you could build an animal out of that wood."

"What kind of animal?" asked Odysseus.

Athena thought for a minute. "Maybe a little horse?"

"**Ooh! Yes!** And pick some grass and flowers for its mane and tail!" added Persephone. She was the goddess girl of plants. Real leaves and flowers grew from her dress and red hair. Four-leaf clovers, too. Zeus had given her the clovers to bring her good luck.

"Great ideas!" said Odysseus. "Thanks! See you all inside later on." He ran off to gather some branches.

The girls returned to the glass wall. The pet show lady wrote Oliver's name on her list. Then she pressed her gold apple to the wall. The apple hummed a tune. The girls all held hands and stepped forward. Right away, the glass began to ripple around them. Then they passed through the magical wall!

4

Pet Show

Now the goddess girls were inside Sparkle City! A gleaming zigzag tower shaped like a giant thunderbolt stood at its center. That was where Zeus lived. Roads stuck out from the base of the tower like spokes on a wagon wheel. Along them stood little shops and houses of different shapes and sizes. Happy, smiling people with pets were everywhere.

The girls began to walk toward the center of town.

"Are you really going to enter Oliver in the pet show?" Artemis asked Athena.

"Yes, do it!" Persephone and Aphrodite said together.

"I will!" said Athena. "After all, that lady outside the wall already put him on her list." She looked at Artemis. "Can you do tricks with him for the show?"

Artemis nodded. **"Sure! That'll be fun!"**

Just then, they passed a pet shop. A talking sign stood out front. "All **grooming** supplies are free today!" it told them. That it could talk was no surprise. Many things could talk in Mount Olympus.

"Hey! We should buy some supplies and get Oliver spiffed up," Aphrodite suggested to the other girls. "There are lots of **awesome** animals here for the show. He should look his best."

They went inside the shop. There, the girls combed Oliver. They clipped his hair. Athena added a cute red bow to his collar. And Persephone tucked some four-leaf clovers into the bow's knot. "For luck," she told him.

When they set Oliver on the ground, he pranced around happily. "I think he likes his new look!" said Artemis.

The goddess girls took to him to the city square. Along the way, Artemis thought of something. Oliver belonged to Athena. So she should be in the show with him too. Not just Artemis.

"I have an idea for tricks Oliver can do, but I'll need your help," she told Athena. She explained her idea as the girls all walked. Persephone and Aphrodite added suggestions too. By the time they reached the city square, they had a good plan.

The square was like a small park next to Zeus's **Thunderbolt Tower**. All the pet owners and their pets were gathered there, waiting for the show to start.

Athena **elbowed** Artemis and pointed. "Look, there's Paris. Holding the pink kitten."

Artemis nodded. She looked around the square. "I wonder if

Odysseus got in. I don't see him. **But there's Zeus!**"

That super-duper powerful godboy sat across the square on a fancy **throne**. It was the same one that had been inside the tower last time they were here. But now it had been moved outside. Zeus

had black hair and wore a **tunic**. There was a shiny thunderbolt on his belt. He was eight years old, the same age as the girls. But he ruled Mount Olympus!

Just then, Zeus stood up. A hush fell over the crowd.

"Welcome to the Sparkle City pet show! There will be twenty pets doing tricks today. And prizes for everyone," he called loudly. **"Now let the pet show begin!"** He sat down.

"I wonder what the prizes will

be," Artemis said to her friends.

Before anyone could guess, Zeus spoke again. "First up is **Pigasus**, the pig poet!" With a whoosh, the winged blue pig they'd seen in line zoomed skyward.

The crowd oohed and aahed as the pig circled above them. Then it said a silly poem:

I like to fly

high in the sky

to make it rain.

Want to know why?

'Cause rain makes mud puddles!

And pigs love mud puddles!

So saying, the pig zoomed toward a rain cloud.

"**Stop!** Don't make it rain right now. Not in the middle of our show!" Zeus called to the pig.

Pigasus looked a bit disappointed. But he obeyed and smiled. After he landed, he went back to

with its owner, a singing skunk sang a song called "We Love to Stink"! A dancing peacock and its owner did the hokey pokey. A pair of pet dragons puffed words in purple smoke. The crowd clapped after each act.

Finally, it was Oliver's turn.

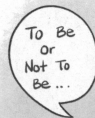

his owner, who hugged him.

Now it was the pom-pom poodle's turn for tricks. She made her two tails wiggle, which made everyone giggle. She could bend them into shapes, too, like question marks.

Next came Skamperoo the kangaroo. *Boing!* It leaped so high, it went clear over Thunderbolt Tower and back again!

After that was Snakespeare, a talking snake that acted out part of a play.

More acts followed. Together

5

Trick Dog

"And last of all we have Oliver the trick dog!" Zeus called out. Oliver trotted out into the middle of the square and sat down. Athena stood next to him.

Artemis stood a few feet away.

She pulled one silver arrow from her quiver. She strung it in her bow. **"Time for tricks!"** she told Oliver and Athena.

Athena nodded.

Oliver nodded too, like he understood.

Artemis pulled back her bow and sent her arrow high into the air. "Spin," she called to the arrow. The arrow stopped in midair and began spinning.

At the same time, the wings on Athena's sandals began to flap.

The magic sandals lifted her off the ground. The white wings at their heels spun her around and around.

Oliver leaped in the air and did a spin too. And another and another. Everyone clapped!

"Now loop-the-loop!" Artemis called to her arrow.

High overhead, the arrow stopped spinning. Now it did a bunch of loop-the-loops. Up in the sky, Athena also did loop-the-loops with her magic sandals' help! Oliver jumped in the air and did loop-the-loops too. The crowd clapped again.

When they finished, Artemis called out, "And now it's time for a bow that will wow!" she told the crowd.

"**Bow!**" she commanded the arrow.

The arrow bent in half as if bowing to the crowd below. Athena bowed to them as well. Oliver stood, then pushed his two front paws out. His head went down. He looked like he was bowing!

He's so cute! thought Artemis. Everyone else must have thought so too. The clapping got even louder.

It was time to finish their act. "Sparkles!" Artemis commanded her arrow.

The arrow flew high over Thunderbolt Tower. It shot sparkly fireworks out of its tip! Everyone cheered!

Athena and Artemis hugged Oliver. "Great job, buddy," they told him. He was so happy with their praise that he wiggled all over.

Grinning, Artemis called back her arrow and put it and her bow away. Persephone and Aphrodite ran out to give the other two girls and Oliver hugs.

"Do you think Oliver has some magic inside him?" wondered Persephone. "Because those tricks of his were extra awesome!"

"Probably. After all, he is from magical Mount Olympus!" said Aphrodite.

Artemis looked around at all the cute, happy pets in the square. "Every one of these pets is awesome. I wish they could all be mine," she said dreamily.

As soon as she spoke these words, the pets all turned to look at her. Like they had somehow heard and understood her! Then they all began coming over to her. All but the kitten. Paris was holding it snug, so it stayed in his arms.

The pets gathered around Artemis so she could pet them

each in turn. They did their tricks for her. The poodle's pom-pom tails curved to make a heart shape at her. The dragons puffed purple smoke hearts that made her sneeze. Pigasus made up a poem for her as he flew in circles over her head:

Roses are red,
pigs are blue.
Artemis, Artemis,
I love you!

The pets' owners came to get them. But the pets wouldn't leave Artemis. She looked at her friends.

"What's going on here? I like animals, and I know they like me. But this is too much!"

Just then, a strange-looking horse galloped into the middle of the city square. Its legs were hidden under a long grass blanket thrown over its back.

"Sorry I'm late for the pet show!" it yelled. Then it snorted and neighed.

Zeus frowned at it. "Who are you? There's no talking horse on my list of pets for the show."

"Who am I? I'll tell you who I am," neighed the horse. Its eyes moved over the crowd as it began to prance around the square. Almost like it was looking for someone.

Athena studied it as it passed them. "I think that horse is made of wood!"

Aphrodite nodded. "Yeah. Branches and sticks held together with long pieces of tree bark."

"And its mane, tail, and blanket are made of grass and flowers," noted Persephone.

"It must be the pet Odysseus made!" said Artemis. **"But where is *he*?"**

The horse trotted around the city square. *Clip-clop! Clip-clop!* When it reached Paris, it came to a sudden stop.

It leaned to one side. Then the horse fell over to lie on the ground.

A boy popped out from under it and waved his arms high. "Surprise! I'm Odysseus, that's who!"

Artemis gasped. "He was wearing a horse costume! One that he made out of those branches and stuff."

Seeing Odysseus hop out, Paris jumped in alarm. This surprised the kitten. She shot out of his arms and raced across the square.

"Nooo!" yelled Paris. "Come back, Helen!"

6

Copycat

Odysseus ran after the cat and grabbed it. **"Gotcha!"** he said. He held the kitten gently against his chest, calming it.

Paris ran up to him. "Give me that kitten. She's mine!" he yelled.

His loud tone scared the kitten again. She pushed off Odysseus's chest and raced away. This time both boys chased after her. They yelled and pushed at each other as they ran.

The kitten dashed toward Zeus. She shot between his legs and hid under his throne. Zeus reached down and scooped her up. He gently set her in his lap.

Zeus petted the kitten. Slowly, she began to calm down. She rubbed her head against his hand and purred.

The boys ran over to the throne. Zeus frowned at them. "What's going on here? Why are you two fighting over this kitten?"

"Her name is Helen. She belongs to my king," Odysseus explained. Then he pointed at Paris. "But he stole her!"

"I did not!" shouted Paris. "I found her on the Hello Brick Road. She was lost. He and his king don't know how to take care of her!" **"That's not true!"** shouted Odysseus.

Zeus thought for a minute. Then

he said, "I know how to settle this fight. I'll put the kitten down. Whichever boy she runs to can keep her."

Zeus set the kitten on the ground. She looked around. Then she ran straight past the boys and over to Artemis. She jumped into her arms! Like all the other animals in the pet show, she seemed to want to be with her. But why?

Artemis held the kitten and petted her. "I don't understand why, but all the pets seem to be in love with me," she told Zeus.

"I see that," said Zeus, studying her. "And you really don't know why this is happening?"

Artemis shook her head.

"It's not her fault they all want to be with her," said Athena.

"They can probably tell she loves them a lot too," said Persephone.

"Yeah," said Aphrodite. She turned to Artemis. "Helen really likes you, goddess girl!"

Odysseus's eyebrows went up in surprise. "Goddess girl?" He looked at Artemis. "You're a goddess?"

Artemis nodded, still cuddling the pink kitten. "Mm-hmm. My friends and I are all goddess girls."

"Uh-oh." Odysseus said. "Did you pet Helen earlier today? And make a wish later on? Something to do with pets?"

"Yes!" Artemis said, wondering how he knew. "I petted her back on the Hello Brick Road. And a few minutes ago, I wished I could have all these pets for my own. But I didn't mean it. Not exactly. I just like animals is all."

Odysseus groaned. "Here's the thing. Helen's not just any kitten. **She's a wishing kitten!**"

"Which means what, exactly?" Zeus asked him.

"It means she's magic," Odysseus said. "If you are a goddess girl or a god boy and you pet her, you will be granted three wishes."

"I should have told you and

your friends that," Odysseus said to Artemis. "Only I didn't know you were goddess girls."

"**Wait!** I'm a god boy. And I was petting her. So do I get three wishes?" Zeus asked hopefully.

Odysseus shook his head. "No, only one person in every new land Helen visits gets three wishes."

"So in Mount Olympus, only Artemis will get wishes? And no one else can wish after her?" asked Aphrodite.

"Right," said Odysseus.

"Is there a way to undo the wish I made?" asked Artemis.

Odysseus nodded. "Just keep holding Helen and say, 'Take away Kitten Wish Number One.'"

"Take away Kitten Wish Number One," Artemis said quickly. Her wish-undo worked! The pets all went back to their owners. All except the kitten. She stayed in her arms.

"This kitten still doesn't seem to know who she belongs to," Athena noted.

"To me!" yelled Paris.

"To my king!" yelled Odysseus.

"What a mess," Zeus grumped.

Luckily, Artemis had an idea. A goddess-worthy idea. She would use the two wishes she had left to fix this!

"Kitten Wish Number Two," she said aloud. **"I wish this kitten had a twin."**

Zing! Suddenly, another kitten appeared in her arms. It was pink, too, and had green eyes. It looked exactly like Helen!

7

All Is Well

Artemis set the two kittens down. They began to run around and chase each other. Soon she lost track of which kitten was which.

So did everyone else. Paris frowned. "I can't tell which one is the *real* Helen. They look exactly the same to me."

Artemis smiled. "Then it won't matter which one you pick. You and Odysseus can both have a kitten now."

"I'll choose first," Odysseus said.

"No way!" said Paris.

"But the kittens are exactly

the same!" said Zeus. He rolled his eyes. "I think you two would find something to fight about no matter what."

"Kitten Wish Number Three!" Artemis said quickly. "I wish Paris and Odysseus would each pick a different kitten and stop fighting."

Instantly, her wish was granted. (Even though it was really two wishes in one.)

Paris picked up a kitten. "I choose this one. I just know she's

Helen." He cuddled the kitten. "Aren't you a sweetie-weetie?"

Odysseus picked up the other kitten. "No way! This is the real Helen. You chose wrong!" He curled the kitten into one arm and petted her until she purred.

Zeus let out a huff. "Just take your kittens, be happy, and go home. I have prizes to give out!"

He stood up from his throne. Then he went around behind it and grabbed a big box. It held many bags tied with bright-colored rib-

bons. He reached in and pulled out bunches of them. He tossed them out into the crowd.

The pets or their owners caught them. Inside the bags were pet toys and treats! There were enough bags for everyone. As the pets enjoyed their prizes, laughter and happy animal sounds filled the city square.

Artemis watched Paris and Odysseus share the new toys and treats with their kittens. Both boys thought they held the real kitten, so both were pleased. Not even she could tell the real kitten from the copycat!

"My king will be so glad to get Helen back," Odysseus told the goddess girls. "He really loves her. He plays with her every day.

She even has her own small royal throne next to his." He turned to leave. "Thanks for your help," he called over his shoulder to the goddess girls. Then he headed back toward the kingdom he'd come from.

"I'll be off now too," Paris told the girls. "I'm going to take Helen to my home here in Sparkle City. It's in a great neighborhood called Troy. I'll build a playroom there, just for her! Thanks for helping," he told the girls. Then he headed off the opposite way from Odysseus.

Once they were gone, the goddess girls grinned at one another. It was good to know both kittens would have good homes.

"All's well that ends well," said a small voice. It was coming from above. The goddess girls looked up. Fluttering in the air near them was a glowing fairylike goddess with wings.

"Hestia!" the goddess girls called out. They smiled at her.

The tiny goddess smiled back.

"Good work today, girls! Both Helens will live happily ever after thanks to you."

To Artemis she said, "That was some smart thinking to wish for a second look-alike kitten!"

Her praise warmed Artemis's heart. "Thanks."

Hestia's glow began to blink on and off. This meant she would soon disappear. She could never visit for long. Speaking quickly, she said to Athena, "It's time for you to take a trip back to your faraway home for a little while. Use your magic sandals. Remember how?"

Athena nodded.

Blink! Before anyone could speak again, the fairylike goddess was gone.

Artemis turned to Athena. "I wish you didn't have to leave Mount Olympus," she said. If she hadn't already used up her Kitten Wish Number Three, maybe this wish could have come true! Still, as sad as she felt, she understood that Athena must be missing her home. It wouldn't be fair to make her stay in Mount Olympus against her will.

Persephone and Aphrodite looked sad too. "I'll miss you so much!" Persephone said to Athena.

"Me too," said Aphrodite.

"And I'll miss all of you!" Athena told her friends. "But don't worry. My sandals can bring me back here anytime."

The four best friends did a
group hug.

"Good luck on your trip home,"
Persephone told Athena.

"Come back soon!"

said Aphrodite.

"I'll take good care of Oliver till you get back," said Artemis.

"Where is he, anyway?" asked Athena.

The girls looked around for him. They laughed when they saw him digging in the box of toys and treats.

It was time for Athena to go. She began to chant the magic words Hestia had given her some time ago:

"Although sometimes friends must part, they're never far away. Home and friends live in your heart. You'll meet again one day!"

When she finished the chant, Athena clicked her sandals' winged heels together three times.

Whoosh! A strong, sparkly wind suddenly whipped up. It lifted Athena off her feet. It blew her high in the sky. She waved and called to her friends. "Goodbye!"

Aphrodite, Persephone, and

Artemis also waved. "Goodbye!"
they called back.

"Woof! Woof!" barked
Oliver as Athena was whisked off
to her faraway home again.

Artemis was sure he was saying goodbye too. "Come, Oliver!" she called to him. He ran over to her, and she picked him up. She hugged him close. "Don't worry," she told him. "Athena will be back again one day."

Persephone nodded. "And I have a feeling it won't be long."

"Yeah," said Aphrodite, "as soon as a new adventure turns up, I expect Athena will too!"

Artemis smiled at the two girls. They were right. Athena was bound to be back soon. And until then, the three of them had one another. Plus Oliver, of course!

She set the little dog down. Then she picked up a shiny red ball. It was one of the new toys Oliver had gotten from Zeus.

Artemis tossed the ball across the square. "Go, boy! Fetch!" she yelled to Oliver.

"Woof!" Wagging his tail, Oliver dashed off to get it.

Word List

accident (AX•ih•dent): Mistake

adores (uh•DOORZ): Loves or really likes something or someone

awesome (AW•sum): Great

curious (KYOOR•ee•us): Interested in learning more about something or someone

elbowed (ELL•bowd): Got someone's attention by poking them with your elbow

gasped (GASPD): Made a surprised sound

goddess (GOD•ess): A girl or

woman with magic powers in Greek mythology

gods (GODZ): Boys or men with magic powers in Greek mythology

Greece (GREES): A country on the continent of Europe

Greek mythology (GREEK mith•AH•luh•jee): Stories people in Greece made up long ago to explain things they didn't understand about their world

grooming (GREWM•ing): Related to brushing, cleaning, and taking care of an animal

Mount Olympus (MOWNT oh•LIHM•puss): Tallest mountain in Greece

praise (PRAYZ): Kind or encouraging words

quiver (QWIV•er): A bag for arrows

spoil (SPOIL): To ruin something

throne (THROWN): A fancy, royal chair

Thunderbolt Tower (THUHN•der•bolt TOW•er): Where Zeus lives in Sparkle City

tunic (TOO•nihk): A knee-length shirt worn by a Greek god

Questions

1. Do you have a pet? If so, what do you like most about it? If you could have a new pet, what kind would you choose?

2. If you could create a silly pet to enter into a pet show, what would you name it? What tricks might it do? Can you draw a picture of your silly pet at the pet show?

3. If you could make three wishes come true, what would they be?

(Make one wish for yourself. Make the other two wishes for others, such as friends, your family, or someone else.)

4. Who is your favorite character in this book? Why? What do you like about them?

5. What do you think Artemis, Persephone, and Aphrodite will do while Athena is gone?

Authors' Note

Most of the ideas and characters in the Little Goddess Girls books come from **Greek mythology**. This book is based on a Greek myth called the Trojan Horse. It's about a trick that a Greek named Odysseus played during a war against Paris and the Trojans. Odysseus wanted to set Queen Helen free from the city of Troy, where Paris lived. Odysseus built and hid inside a big wooden horse.

When the Trojans came near, he and his army jumped out. They surprised the Trojans and won the war.

We were also inspired by *The Wishing Horse of Oz*. It is the twenty-ninth in the Oz books series created by L. Frank Baum. And we added lots of fun, friendship, and girl power!

We hope you enjoy reading all the Little Goddess Girls books!

—*Joan Holub and Suzanne Williams*